Farm Animals

by Heidi Daniel

Strategy Focus

As you read, think about what you want to know about the animals.

 HOUGHTON MIFFLIN   BOSTON

My Words

big

huge

small

tall

tiny

A mouse is tiny.

A chicken is small.

A horse is big.

A duck is small.

A cow is huge.

A donkey is tall.